Disney's
My Very First Winnie the Pooh™

Tiggers Hate to Lose

Adapted by
Cassandra Case

Illustrated by
Josie Yee

SCHOLASTIC INC.

New York Toronto London Auckland Sydney
Mexico City New Delhi Hong Kong Buenos Aires

Published by Scholastic Inc., 90 Old Sherman Turnpike, Danbury, CT 06816
by arrangement with Disney Licensed Publishing.

SCHOLASTIC and associated logos are trademarks
and/or registered trademarks of Scholastic Inc.

ISBN 0-7172-8924-9

Printed in the U.S.A.

It was a fine spring morning, and Tigger had been out in the meadow practicing some new, springy bounces. As he came along beside the stream, Tigger saw Pooh and some of his other Hundred-Acre Wood friends standing on the bridge. They were all staring down into the water.

"Hoo-hoo-hoo! Hey! Whatcha watchin'?" Tigger asked, bouncing up onto the bridge.

"We're playing Pooh-sticks," squeaked Piglet.

"Oh, good! Tiggers love Pooh-sticks!" said Tigger. "What's Pooh-sticks?"

"It's a game," answered Pooh. "If you go find yourself some sticks, you can play, too."

"Okey-dokey," said Tigger. "I'll go and get 'em!"

igger went down the path next to the bridge and found some sticks. Then he bounced back to the others.

"What's next?" he asked.

So Rabbit explained: "Now everyone throws a stick into the water on one side of the bridge, and the first stick to pass under the bridge to the other side wins. On your mark, get set . . . go!"

Pooh, Piglet, Rabbit, Roo, and Eeyore all threw their sticks into the water. Rabbit's counting took Tigger by surprise, so he didn't throw his stick in time.

"I'm just watchin' this time, anyways," said Tigger.

Tigger watched while they all raced to the other side of the bridge to see whose stick would win.

"I can see mine!" Roo shouted. "I win! I win!"

But just as he said the words, Roo's "stick" startled them all by flying up into the air! Everybody gasped.

Then Rabbit started to laugh. "It's a dragonfly, Roo! That wasn't your stick."

"I can't see mine," said Piglet. "Can you see yours, Pooh?"

"No, I can't see mine, either," Pooh replied. "I expect my stick is stuck."

"Look!" Rabbit cried. "There's Eeyore's stick!"

"Oh, joy," mumbled Eeyore. "What do you know . . . I won."

"All right, everybody, step aside," Tigger said. "Now I'll show you how great tiggers are at Pooh-sticks."

Everyone moved over so Tigger could play, too. They all lined up along one side of the bridge, and once again Rabbit gave the signal.

"On your mark, get set . . . go!"

They all tossed their sticks off the bridge.

Tigger used an extra bouncy way of throwing that he had just made up. He was sure it would make his stick go the fastest.

Then everyone raced to the other side.

"I won!" shouted Tigger, even before he got to the other side. "Didn't I win?"

"Nope," said Eeyore. "I'm afraid not, Tigger. Here comes my stick now."

Eeyore won again.

"Oh, well . . . ," said Tigger, frowning. "I was just warmin' up, anyways, so it doesn't count. I haven't been doin' too much throwin' lately. Let's play again."

So they played again. But just like before, Eeyore's stick sailed past the others.

"Yes, that's really my stick," said Eeyore. "How very interesting."

"It's not innerestin'!" complained Tigger. "It's a trick of the water."

"And it's no fair!" said Tigger, stamping his foot. "Tiggers hate to lose. I wanna play again."

Eeyore won the next game, too.

"Four times in a row," Eeyore said. "Who would ever have thought it."

They played again, and Eeyore won again.

"Fascinating!" mumbled Eeyore as he picked up his stick. "Just plain fascinating."

And Eeyore won the time after that, too.

"I just don't seem to be able to lose," Eeyore muttered to himself. "I've won each time."

But Tigger jumped up and down and shouted, "Tiggers aren't s'posed to lose! They aren't made that way. We have to play again."

So they played another game.

This time Tigger's stick was out in front! But at the very last moment, Eeyore's stick edged ahead of Tigger's and won.

Tigger threw down his sticks. "Tiggers do NOT like Pooh-sticks!" he yelled.

Tigger's throat felt tight, and his eyes began to prickle, and he wanted to go home. He walked away with his head down.

The sun was shining and it was still a fine spring day, but Tigger had no bounce at all.

"I know how you feel," said Eeyore, who was suddenly beside him.

"Huh?" said Tigger.

"Usually it's me who loses," explained Eeyore. "But Christopher Robin told me something out of a book: 'It's not whether you win or lose. It's how you play the game.'"

"Well, how do you play it, then?" asked Tigger.

"Just have fun playing and don't worry who wins," said Eeyore. "But, I'll tell you a secret," he whispered. "That is . . . if you want to know."

"'Course I wanna know!" said Tigger.

"Come to the bridge, Tigger," said Eeyore.

Tigger didn't feel like playing Pooh-sticks again, but he was curious.

"See, I drop my stick in a twitchy sort of way," Eeyore explained, showing Tigger how.

Next, Eeyore dropped a stick *without* twitching while Tigger tried the twitchy way.

And this time, Tigger's stick won!

"Hoo-hoo! I won!" cried Tigger, beginning to bounce again.

"Oh . . . it's not whether ya spin or snooze," sang Tigger, "it's how ya play the game, hoo-hoo!"

"Amazing!" muttered Eeyore. "It really does work." Then he smiled and said, "Thank you, Tigger."

"What for?" Tigger asked as he bounced.

"For helping me prove that my discovery really works," Eeyore replied.

"You're the bestest pal, Eeyore ol' buddy," cried Tigger, giving Eeyore a bouncy hug.

"I am?" asked Eeyore.

"Yes indeedy! 'Cause even though tiggers hate ta lose, it still can be fun just playin' the game with a friend like you. Hoo-hoo!"